NORTHERN
LIGHTS BOOKS FOR CHILDREN

The Most Beautiful Kite in the World

Georgia Graham

by Andrea Spalding

Illustrations by Georgia Graham

PUBLISHED BY

RED DEER COLLEGE PRESS

The Most Beautiful Kite in the World

Credits
Edited for the Press by Dennis Johnson
Design: Robert MacDonald, MediaClones Inc.,
Toronto Ontario and Banff Alberta
Printed in Hong Kong

Northern Lights Books for Children are published by
Red Deer College Press
56 Avenue & 32 Street, Box 5005
Red Deer Alberta Canada T4N 5H5

Canadian Cataloguing in Publication Data
Spalding, Andrea.
The most beautiful kite in the world
(Northern lights books for children)
ISBN 0-88995-053-9
I. Pow Graham, Georgia. II. Title. III. Series.
PS8587.P34M6 1988   jc813'.54   C88-091022-4
PZ7.S634Mo 1988

For my father
who made my first kite.
-Andrea Spalding

To my daughter Paige who has
brought so much joy into my life.
-Georgia Graham

Jenny ran quickly down the road towards the school. If she ran fast, she had one whole minute to spend inside the General Store. One whole minute to look at the most beautiful kite in the world.

"Excuse me, how much is the big red kite?" she asked the storekeeper.

"Five dollars and ninety-five cents," he answered.

Jenny frowned. She had only seventy-five cents in her piggy bank, but tomorrow was her birthday. Maybe her father would buy her the red kite as a present.

The school bell rang, and she skipped carefully down the sidewalk avoiding all the cracks and humming to herself.

"Step on a crack,
Break your back;
Take a hike,
Fly a kite."

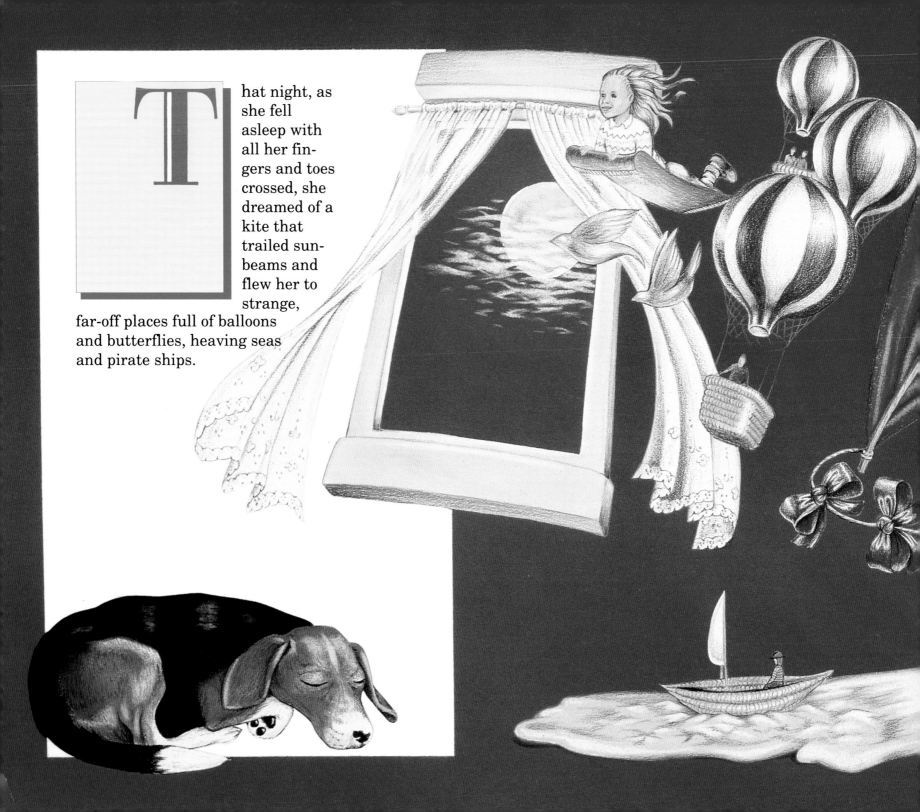

T hat night, as she fell asleep with all her fingers and toes crossed, she dreamed of a kite that trailed sunbeams and flew her to strange, far-off places full of balloons and butterflies, heaving seas and pirate ships.

Her birthday dawned, golden and gusty.

"Perfect kite weather!" she thought and jumped out of bed, hurriedly dressed and ran into the kitchen.

There was a kite-shaped parcel by her breakfast bowl. Jenny ripped off the wrapping paper in long strips.

It was a kite. But not the big red one from the store, not the kite of her dream. This was a home-made one. She recognized the light wood from her father's workshed. He must have worked while she was asleep, shaping the frame and covering it with white paper.

Her throat felt tight and dry.

Her father came into the kitchen whistling. "Good morning, Jenny. I see you've found your present. Like it?"

Jenny smiled, but her lips quivered. Her throat hurt too much to speak, but she ran over and gave him a big, hard hug.

"Eat your breakfast," he said happily, "and we'll go out and see how your kite flies."

The food stuck in Jenny's throat. She only nodded.

hey walked out into the spring sunshine. Her father had a bounce in his step, but Jenny's feet felt like lead, and her eyes watered.

"It's the dust," she explained.

Her father took a roll of string from his pocket and helped Jenny attach it to her kite.

"I'll hold the kite while you let out the string," he instructed. "Then, when I shout, run into the wind."

Jenny waited while he carried the kite several paces away and held it up to the breeze.

"Ready, Jenny? Run!"

Jenny ran. But the kite only swooped and dragged in the prairie grass. She sighed with disappointment.

"Hmm," said her father, "that's what I need to know. It's nose heavy, needs a tail." He tied a loose piece of string to the bottom of the kite. "Look around, Jenny. See if you can find anything to make bows for the tail."

Jenny scuffed her shoes in the dirt. *"Why should the kite need bows and tail?"* she thought. *"The red kite would have flown perfectly the first time."*

On a nearby porch sat their neighbour, Mrs. Omelchuk. She was knitting a yellow sweater and enjoying the early morning sunshine. Jenny walked slowly over.

"Please could you spare me some wool? I need to tie bows on the tail of my kite."

Mrs. Omelchuk gave her a big yellow handful. Jenny took it to her father and stood back to watch him tie three bows that gleamed like sunbeams.

"That will never work," she thought disgustedly.

"Come on, Jenny. Let's try again." Her father held the kite high above his head. "Are you ready with the string? Run!"

This time Jenny felt the string lift as she sped into the wind, and she glanced back hopefully. But a moment later the kite fell to the prairie. It was still nose heavy. Jenny stamped her foot.

"I knew it wouldn't work. This kite will never fly," she cried in frustration.

Her father came over and placed his arm around her shoulders. "Sure it will," he reassured her. "We just need more bows to balance it."

"Really? That's all it needs?" asked Jenny. She looked thoughtfully at the kite. It *had* flown better the second time, and the wool from Mrs. Omelchuk did look pretty.

Her father smiled and ruffled her hair. "Yup, that's all. Just two or three more bows..."

"And WHOoooOSH, up it goes!" Jenny laughed.

And she ran off to find them.

r. Braun was reading a magazine with a bright red cover. Jenny bounced up to him and cleared her throat. He grinned at her.

"Excuse me, but I'm trying to get my kite to fly."

"You need help, liebchen?"

"We need bows for the tail, and I thought…" Jenny hesitated. "Do you need the cover for your magazine?" She blushed.

"I flew kites when I was little. They were fun." Mr. Braun gave her the red cover.

"Oh, thank you, thank you!" Jenny ran to her father waving the cover triumphantly. "Dad, let's try this."

Carefully tearing the paper, they knelt together and added two more bows to the tail. Once more, her father held the kite up.

"Ready, Jenny?"

Jenny nodded eagerly and turned into the wind. She ran swifter and surer than before. The kite quivered and rose for a minute. Then the wind dropped, and it fell, smack, to the ground.

"Oh, rats!"

**H**er father pretended he had not heard. He picked up the kite and balanced it thoughtfully. "One more bow should do it."

Jenny looked around. A movement caught her eye. Leaning against a truck, her friend Charlie was peeling a purple wrapper from an all-day sucker.

"Hey Charlie," she yelled. "Trade you a fly of my kite for that paper off your sucker."

"Doesn't fly yet." Charlie stuck the sucker in his mouth.

"It will if we tie another bow on the tail."

"Well...I guess so." Charlie passed Jenny the wrapper, sauntered over and watched.

Jenny tied the purple bow to the tail, handed the kite to her father and eagerly held the string. Once more he lifted the kite to the breeze.

"One, two, three...Now!"

Jenny ran. Her feet sped lightly over the grass.

Slowly and uncertainly, the kite rose, dipped, then caught the air current and soared upward. Jenny turned, feeling the string come alive.

"Quick! Let out more string," called her father.

She carefully unreeled. The kite pulled and climbed and responded. Jenny's face filled with an enormous grin.

There above her, soaring, dipping and playing tag with a meadowlark, was a magical sight. The early morning brightness caught the kite, held it and turned it to dazzling gold. It was Jenny's dream kite! A sunbeam golden kite that swept the sky with a tail of bobbing yellow, red and purple butterflies.

round her gathered her father and Charlie, then Mrs. Omelchuk and Mr. Braun. They all looked up in wonder.

"Ooh," they said, "how beautiful."

"Yes," beamed Jenny. "It's the most beautiful kite in the world," and she floated across the prairie with her feet barely touching the earth.

The next day, Jenny ran quickly down the road, past the General Store, to the school. If she ran fast, she had one whole minute before the bell rang. One whole minute to show her friends the most beautiful kite in the world.

Acknowledgements

The Publisher gratefully acknowledges
the financial assistance of the Canada
Council, the Alberta Foundation for the
Literary Arts, Alberta Culture, and Red
Deer College.
The audio cassette of *The Most Beautiful
Kite in the World* was made possible, in
part, by a grant from the Alberta Founda-
tion for the Performing Arts through
monies provided by Alberta Lotteries.
The Publisher and Author extend sincere
appreciation.

the
Alberta
Foundation
for the
Performing
Arts

The Publisher and Illustrator
extend special thanks to
Emmy and Bill Stuebing for their kind
assistance.